valenty na Barlow

Eugene Boutenko

valentyna Barlow

James Fenimore Cooper

THE LAST OF
THE MOHICANS

TORMONT

North American Indians in Colonial Times.

Blackfoot Indians on a journey. A sled is attached to their horse for carrying personal belongings or wounded braves.

A Mohawk warrior

A Seminole totem pole

An old Cheyenne chief

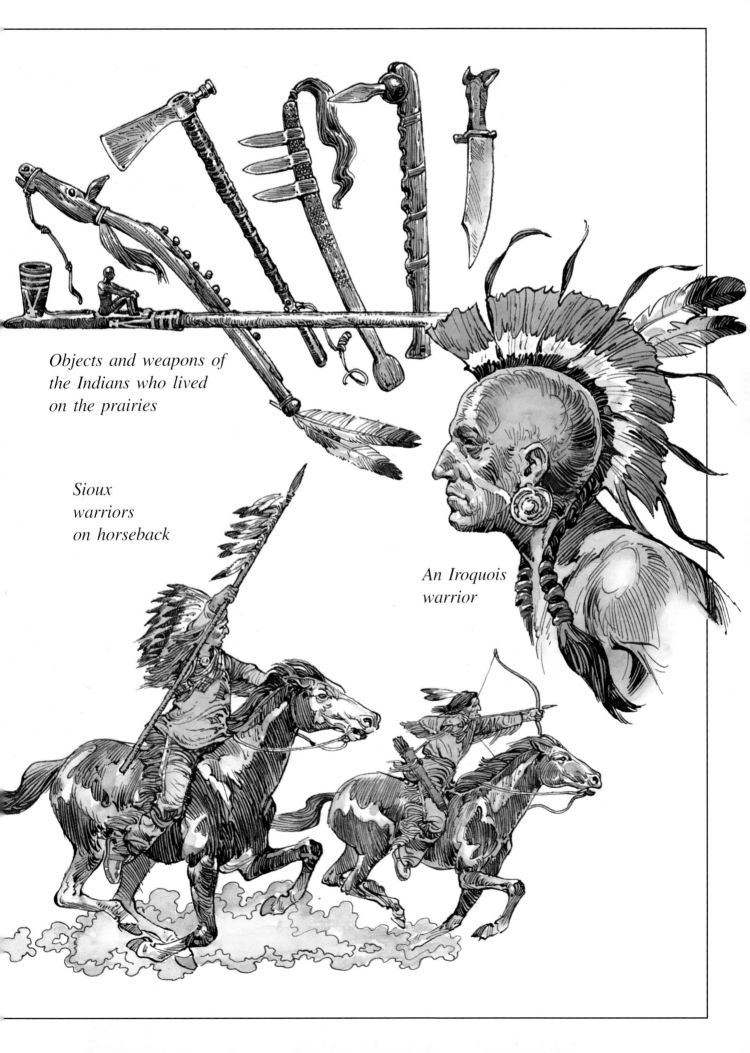

Objects and weapons of the Indians who lived on the prairies

Sioux warriors on horseback

An Iroquois warrior

THE AUTHOR: JAMES FENIMORE COOPER

James Fenimore Cooper was born in 1789 in the United States, and died in 1851. As a young boy, he lived in the wilderness, on the frontier between settlers' land and the Indian territories.

New readers will be surprised to learn that the frontier described in our story was the mountainous Adirondack region of New York State. Nowadays, this is a popular resort area. It was here that the author's father, Judge William Cooper, started a pioneer village.

Young James was a good student, but also a bit of a troublemaker. In fact, he ended up being expelled from school because he blew up his teacher's door by putting gunpowder in the keyhole!

Cooper went to Yale College when he was seventeen. His love of mischief soon ended his college days, and he became a sailor on a merchant vessel. He then joined the United States Navy as a midshipman.

When Cooper was twenty-two, he decided to leave the navy. He married and settled down to a quiet life in the country. One evening, when he was thirty years old, his wife dared him to write a novel. After one or two tries, he began to write tales of frontier days.

Readers all over North America and Europe loved these tales of early pioneering days. They were also fascinated by Cooper's detailed descriptions of American Indians and their customs.

*Cooper wrote thirty novels, including **The Last of the Mohicans,** published in 1826. This is the most famous of his "Leatherstocking Tales" about the heroic adventures of a frontier scout named Natty Bumpo — otherwise known as Hawkeye.*

***The Last of the Mohicans** takes place in the 1750s, when the British and the French were at war in North America.*

The Colonel's Daughters

The summer sun was shining brightly as Cora and Alice packed for a journey through the forest. Their father, Colonel Munro, had sent an Indian runner with a message asking his daughters to join him at Fort William Henry.

The war between the English and French in the colonies was growing fiercer by the day, and the colonel was worried. Wouldn't the girls be safer with him on Lake George, instead of on the Hudson River at Fort Edward?

The two sisters were ready for their journey at dawn the next morning. They would be taken to their father by Duncan Heyward, a young English officer.

Cora waited quietly, her glossy black braids tucked modestly under a dark shawl. Blue-eyed Alice, the younger of the two, tossed her fair hair and smiled cheerfully as Heyward helped her into the saddle.

As the travelers left the fort, Magua, the Indian runner, came forward. "I will show you the short way," he said. "I know the trail."

"I don't like the way that Indian keeps staring at you," whispered Alice to her sister.

"Our father knows this Indian," said Cora. "He must be trustworthy."

Major Heyward accepted Magua's offer, being anxious to make the journey as quickly as possible.

The three riders and their Indian guide left the road and made their way along the forest trail. Suddenly, they heard the sound of hooves clip-clopping over the rough path behind them. The whole party came to a halt. Who could be following them?

A Strange Traveler

Suddenly, a skinny fellow appeared, jogging along on a tired horse. He looked like a clown with his floppy hat, bright yellow trousers, and blue jacket. Something – a sword, perhaps? – stuck out of his pocket.

"Are you looking for someone?" Heyward asked.

"I hear you're going to Fort William Henry. I'm going there myself. David Gamut's my name."

"Why are you going there?" said Heyward.

Gamut didn't answer, but pulled the mysterious weapon from his pocket and held up – a flute!

"A music teacher!" cried Alice with a laugh. She turned to Heyward. "Please let him come along."

Heyward found it hard to refuse, and so the funny-looking fellow joined the little group. The travelers set off again along the woodland trail.

A few miles further west, two men were crouched by the banks of a fast-running river. They spoke in hushed, anxious voices.

The first man was Chingachgook, an Indian. His naked chest bore a fearsome Death Spirit tattoo – a jawless skull, half white, half black. His head was shaved, except for a tuft of hair decorated with a hawk's feather. A tomahawk and scalping-knife were stuck in his belt, and a gun lay across his knees.

The other was a white man, a scout known as Hawkeye to his friends and Long Rifle to his enemies. He wore buckskin clothes, Indian moccasins, and a cap made of animal skins. Against a nearby tree leaned a long hunter's rifle.

"We Mohicans of the Delaware nation were once a happy people," said Chingachgook, speaking his Indian language. "We had buried the tomahawk and lived in peace. Then the white man brought fire-water. My brothers drank it, and foolishly thought they had found the Great Spirit."

The Indian sighed. "They parted with their land. I, a chief of my people, have never seen the graves of my fathers. All my family are gone. My son Uncas is the last of the Mohicans."

"Who speaks of Uncas?" A young warrior slipped between the two men and sat down on the river bank.

"Are there Hurons in these woods, Uncas?" asked Chingachgook.

"I have been on their trail," said the young Indian, "But now they lie hidden, like cowards."

Chingachgook turned to Hawkeye. "Tomorrow we will show them we are men." Then suddenly he jumped up and listened.

"What do you hear, Chingachgook?" said Hawkeye.

The Indian put his ear to the ground. "The white man's horses are coming."

Soon Hawkeye could hear the clatter of hooves. "Who goes there?" cried the scout in English.

"Friends!" called Heyward as he came along the path. "We've come from Fort Edward. How far is Fort William Henry from here?"

Hawkeye snorted. "Hah! You're on the wrong trail, my friend. Why didn't you take the main road?"

"We trusted to an Indian guide, but now it seems we're lost."

"What? An Indian lost in the woods!" cried Hawkeye, shaking his head. "Doesn't he know the deer paths? Is he a Mohawk?"

"I believe he's a Huron adopted by the Mohawks," said Heyward.

"If you ask me, those Hurons are still loyal to the French," Hawkeye muttered.

"Enough!" said Heyward impatiently. "I'm escorting Colonel Munro's daughters to Fort William Henry. You can come with us, if you like."

"I heard a troop was to leave Fort Edward this morning for Lake George," remarked Hawkeye. "Why did you travel with this Huron?"

"I preferred the shorter path," Heyward said.

"And he deserted you?"

"No. He's at the rear."

Hawkeye walked back up the trail and found Magua standing apart, with a rifle folded in his arms. The Huron glared savagely at the scout, who held the Indian's gaze steadily for a moment, then returned to Heyward.

"He's a Huron all right – fierce, cunning, and probably a spy for the French. Lucky thing you met up with us when you did! I'll guide you, but first we must get hold of this devil."

The scout called to his Indian friends, and the three held a whispered conference. A minute later, the Mohicans laid down their rifles and slipped into the underbrush.

"Now, sir," said Hawkeye to Major Heyward, "try to keep that Huron's mind busy, but don't make any move to take him. My Mohican friends will lay hold of him before he knows what's up."

Major Heyward rode back along the trail to the Huron guide. "Magua, night is coming on and we're still a long way from Fort William Henry. Luckily, we've met a hunter who can find us shelter for the night."

"Then Magua will leave! The palefaces will be alone!"

"Colonel Munro won't be pleased," retorted Heyward. "Come, let's not quarrel. Sit down and eat something. We can move on when the young ladies have rested."

The Indian studied Heyward's face suspiciously, then sat down and

took some corn from his pouch. Heyward dismounted and moved slowly toward Magua, talking in a friendly tone.

"Magua," said Heyward, "your corn looks dried out. Maybe I can find you something better."

Magua held out his pouch to the Englishman. Their hands touched. The Indian waited quietly. But when Magua felt Heyward's hand move softly up his arm, he struck it away with a piercing yell, and darted off into the forest. The next instant, Chingachgook and Uncas glided across the trail in swift pursuit.

THE ESCAPE

For a moment, Heyward was so surprised that he couldn't move. Then the sharp crack of a rifle split the air. He ran toward the sound, but before he had gone a hundred yards he met Hawkeye and the Mohicans coming back.

"Why have you given up? We might still catch him!" exclaimed Heyward.

"Are you so tired of life?" snapped the scout. "If we don't get a move on, our scalps will be drying in a Huron camp by morning. Will you follow me?"

"Yes," gasped Heyward, now desperately anxious for the safety of Cora and Alice. Cruel faces seemed to lurk behind every tree as the little band filed down the steep, rocky bank to the river.

Silently, the Indians drew the horses under an overhanging cliff and tied them to bushes by the water-side. Hawkeye pulled a canoe from a hiding place among the bushes and signaled to Heyward and the women to climb in. The scout stepped nimbly aboard, and began to guide the canoe through the swift current with a long pole.

The frail craft raced through the whirling waters. At last, Hawkeye guided it into a quiet pool beside a low, flat rock.

"Wait here," he ordered. "I'll soon be back with the Mohicans and your flute-playing friend."

At last the whole party was on the rock. The Mohicans led the way into an opening in the cliff above the river. To the travelers' amazement, they found themselves in a large cavern. There they spent the night, safe from the dangers of the forest.

THE HURONS ATTACK!

But with the coming of dawn, the travelers' peaceful rest was broken. Hawkeye, keeping watch, was startled by a shrill cry from the woods across the river. The Huron war whoop! The scout stood frozen for a moment, then rushed into the cavern and shook Major Heyward awake. "We must leave at once. Wake up the young ladies and get ready."

As the party clambered down to the shore, bright gunpowder flashes burst from the trees across the river.

"Take cover!" yelled Hawkeye. His companions were already scrambling behind the nearest tree or rock. They returned fire with a blind volley of rifle shots, and the battle raged from shore to shore.

Hawkeye picked up a bullet that had missed him by inches, shook his head and said, "That's strange. It almost seems as if this bullet was shot from above."

"Look!" said Uncas, pointing to a large oak tree that grew high on the river bank. Among its branches crouched an Indian. Hawkeye and Uncas took careful aim. Their rifles fired at the same moment. The Indian's body jerked violently and spun through the air, tumbling into the river beneath.

Hawkeye shook his head, "That was the last of my powder, Uncas. Go down to the canoe and bring me my other powder horn."

Soon after, Uncas gave a shout from the shore. Their small canoe was floating down the river, guided by a Huron swimming alongside it.

"What will to happen to us now?" cried Heyward.

"Our enemies will come sooner or later," said Hawkeye.

"Chingachgook, my brother," he added, turning to the Mohican, "we're about to fight our last battle."

"No!" cried Cora. "You've already done enough for us. You must flee!"

"We could save ourselves," retorted Hawkeye, "but that's not our way. We'd never desert our friends. How could we face your father when he asked us where you were and why we had abandoned you?"

"You *must* go!" insisted Cora. "Find my father and tell him to rescue us."

"The girl's talking sense," muttered Hawkeye. He called the two Mohicans to him.

Chingachgook listened carefully, nodding his head. He crept toward the riverbank. With a wave of an arm to show the direction he was taking, he dove into the water and disappeared.

The Capture

Hawkeye turned to Cora. "If the Hurons take you into the forest, make sure you leave some trace of where you go." He shook the girl's hand warmly, then took his rifle and hid it in a crevice. This done, he crept to the water's edge and slipped into the river. Uncas wasn't slow to follow. Now the travelers were alone.

Brave Cora tried to convince Heyward to escape as well. "Please go, I beg of you!" she said. But the officer refused.

In desperation, Cora dragged Alice to the back of the cavern, followed by Gamut and the major. Heyward tried to camouflage the entrance with several branches. The little group sat quietly, hardly breathing.

They hadn't long to wait. Very soon Indian voices could be heard drawing closer.

"Long Rifle! Long Rifle!" came a cry. The savages had found Hawkeye's rifle, and now they were looking for the body of their hated enemy.

The Indians searched among the rocks, but there was no sign of a body. Suddenly a triumphant whoop rang out. Magua had found the entrance to the cave! In a moment the travelers' refuge was invaded by Hurons, who dragged their victims into the open and surrounded them.

Magua stood a short distance away, staring grimly at the prisoners. "The Hurons want to kill Long Rifle," he said coldly. "If you don't tell them where he is, they will kill you instead."

"He has escaped," answered Heyward.

Magua shook his head in disbelief. "Is Long Rifle a bird that can fly?" he asked mockingly.

"Maybe he's a fish. Long Rifle is a good swimmer!" retorted Heyward.

Several Hurons rushed to the river bank. They ran along the shore, but there was no trace of Hawkeye.

At last, the Indians gave up the search. The prisoners were forced into a canoe and taken across the river by Magua, while the rest of the band swam to the opposite shore.

Here the Hurons split up. The prisoners remained with several Indians led by Magua. The Hurons had discovered the horses, and the group now set off, the girls riding while the others walked alongside. Remembering Hawkeye's advice, Cora cautiously broke a branch every now and then.

The Indians and their captives crossed a valley and started to climb up a hill. It was so steep that Magua forced the two girls to walk.

At the top of the hill they found themselves in a dense forest. Here Magua stopped and beckoned to Cora.

"What can Magua have to say to the daughter of Colonel Munro?" said Cora disdainfully.

"Hear me!" ordered the Indian. "Magua was born a chief among the Red Hurons from the Great Lakes. Then your French brothers came into the forest and taught him to drink fire-water. The other chiefs chased him away to where the British live. There, Gray Head, your father, had me whipped like a dog because I drank fire-water."

"So!" exclaimed Cora. "You want to revenge yourself on helpless women for this insult? Why don't you face him yourself, like a true warrior?"

"Why should Magua risk the rifles of Gray Head's warriors when he has his daughters captive?"

"Well, coward, what do you want?" demanded Cora.

"The daughter of the English chief must follow me and live in my wigwam. The body of Gray

Head may sleep safely among his cannons, but his heart will always be with you, at the mercy of my knife."

"Monster! You live up to your name as a traitor!" cried Cora, white with anger.

The Indian stared at the girl with a cunning smile, then waved her away. Soon he was conferring with the other warriors. Although the prisoners could not understand their language, they were afraid that Magua was planning to kill them.

The Return of Long Rifle

How right they were! Suddenly, the Indians jumped up and threw themselves on their captives. In a few seconds the victims found themselves tied to trees.

Despite her terror, Cora managed to tell Alice and Major Heyward of Magua's terrible threat. They answered just as she had expected: they would rather die than let her make such a sacrifice.

It looked as though their brave promise would soon be tested. An Indian lifted his tomahawk and was about to attack Alice. At that moment, a rifle shot rang out.

The Indian fell to the ground.

"Long Rifle!" the Hurons yelled in horror.

Hawkeye rushed at them, hitting his enemies left and right with the butt of his rifle. Chingachgook followed, and then Uncas. The last of the Mohicans was as agile as a deer. He leapt into the middle of a group of cowering Hurons, waving his tomahawk and giving his blood-curdling war cry.

The Huron chief grabbed a long knife and threw himself on Chingachgook. The fight was fierce but short. Magua wrested himself from the Mohican's grip, and the Hurons fled.

"We never thought we'd see you so soon," Heyward said to Hawkeye. "Where are Colonel Munro's troops?"

"We never reached the fort," said Hawkeye. "We decided it would be better to follow you and Magua, and wait for the best moment to attack."

After a short rest, Hawkeye and the others started off on their journey once more. They reached the banks of a small stream and slowly began to climb a steep hill. When they finally got to the top, they could see Fort William Henry on the plain below.

THE FALL OF FORT WILLIAM HENRY

On a strip of land between the shore of Lake George and the hill was a sight that chilled their hearts.

Hundreds of white military tents dotted the plain.

"We're too late!" said the scout. "Montcalm, the French general, has set up a regular siege and has probably filled the woods with his Indian allies. Luckily for us, there's a fog rolling in. We'll use it as cover and try to enter the fort."

When they reached the grassland at the foot of the hill, the fog grew so thick that they could hardly see one another.

Suddenly a voice came through the mist – a French voice: *"Qui vive?"*

"A friend of France," answered Major Heyward in French.

"You sound like an enemy of France. Stop! Sound the alarm! *Tirez*!"

The order was immediately carried out. At least fifty rifle shots crackled all around them, but the fog was so thick that not a single bullet found its mark.

Suddenly the thunder of a cannon could be heard.

Hawkeye and his friends began to run toward the cannon, with the French on their heels.

"Get ready, men!" yelled a voice above them.

"Father! Father!" cried Alice, recognizing Colonel Munro's voice. Without realizing it, they had arrived beneath the tall stockade surrounding the fort.

A tall, stout officer hurried through the fog. "Cora! Alice!" shouted their father. He hugged them tightly while tears rolled down his cheeks. "Thank the Lord! Now I can face anything!"

The colonel knew that the fort was in great danger.

There was hardly any gunpowder left after several day's siege, and Munro had only a small number of soldiers in his garrison. The French force from Canada had thousands of men.

Munro decided to send Hawkeye to Fort Edward for help. The scout crept away through the woods. Late the next day, the scout was led into the French camp, his hands bound!

Montcalm's troops had captured Hawkeye as he returned from his mission. In his pocket they found a letter from General Webb at Fort Edward. Montcalm sent Hawkeye back to Munro, asking for a meeting.

"I'll meet him without hesitation," said Munro, "as befits an officer of King George!"

An Honorable Surrender

Colonel Munro and Major Heyward left the fort and entered Montcalm's tent. The French general was the first

to break the silence. "I am asking for your surrender. Your men have fought bravely, but I've observed your fort carefully. I know all its weak points."

"Ask the French general if he can see Fort Edward through his spyglass," said Munro to Heyward, who was serving as interpreter. "And does he realize that General Webb's regiment is on its way?"

"Why don't we let General Webb answer your question?" replied Montcalm, handing Munro the captured letter.

The colonel grabbed the paper. His face fell as he read. Instead of encouraging Munro to resist, General Webb advised him to surrender immediately. The general couldn't send any troops to help.

"I see that we have no choice," said Munro.

"You won't be able to save the fort," replied the French general. "We must destroy it, of course, but you and your brave soldiers deserve the most honorable terms of surrender."

Montcalm was as good as his word. The fort was to be handed over to the enemy the next morning, but the entire British force could leave, taking its weapons and flags. To surrender a flag would have been a great dishonor.

However, Montcalm refused to provide an armed escort for the small garrison.

At dawn, Heyward visited Cora and Alice. He found them ready, but afraid of making another forest journey.

SAVED BY A SONG

Heyward reassured the two sisters as best he could. He asked David Gamut to watch over them.

No sooner had the column of departing soldiers and civilians entered the forest than nearly three thousand shrieking savages swooped down upon them.

Munro's two daughters were quickly surrounded by a group of Hurons. Cora and Alice clung to each other as a Huron raised a tomahawk. Before it could fall, however, a strange sound rose through the air. David Gamut had pushed himself between the Huron and his victims and was bellowing a hymn as loudly as he could.

The Indians were at first amazed, then terrified by the chanting of unknown words. "Houah!" they yelled, backing off from this strange white witchdoctor.

The song caught Magua's sharp ears. Cora trembled as she saw the hated figure.

"Come, woman!" shouted Magua. "The Huron's wigwam is still open to you!"

"I'd rather die!" cried Cora.

Magua hesitated for a moment. Then he saw Alice, who had fainted. He snatched her up and ran off.

"Wait!" screamed Cora. She ran after her kidnapped sister, and Gamut followed as Magua went deeper and deeper into the forest.

The slaughter by the Hurons was terrible. For three days, no one realized that Cora and Alice weren't dead. Hawkeye, Munro, and Heyward followed the Mohicans as they began to pick up Magua's traces.

The trail led them to an Indian village near a small lake. The would-be rescuers backed off cautiously. Suddenly Heyward heard leaves rustling behind him. He turned to find himself a few steps away from a strange-looking Indian.

This remarkable savage was a scrawny individual. His head was shaved except for a lock of hair from which three or four faded feathers dangled.

Hawkeye started to laugh. "Well, friend, do you want to teach the beavers to sing, too?"

The strange savage was David Gamut!

"Where are Cora and Alice?" asked Heyward anxiously.

"They're prisoners of the savages. Magua took Cora to the Delaware tribe for safekeeping. Alice is here, being watched over by Huron women."

"But why do they let you roam around like this?" asked the other.

"It's all thanks to my hymns," replied Gamut.

Hawkeye smiled. "Indians never hurt anyone who's crazy! I think you should let Alice know we're here."

"I want to go with him," said Heyward.

"All right," said Hawkeye, "let's see what we can do."

Chingachgook painted Heyward's face with the markings of a traveling witchdoctor, and made him a headdress of fur and feathers. Hawkeye exchanged his buckskin clothes and moccasins for the officer's outfit, and the new medicine man was ready.

Heyward and Gamut set off for the village.

As soon as the children playing around the huts saw the two men, they started yelling. Gamut was used to this, and kept on walking toward the village council lodge.

Heyward followed him inside and sat down on the ground. "I come from Canada," he said in French to the council members. "The French king, our White Father, has sent me to his children, the Red Hurons from the Great Lakes. I am to ask if any are sick."

A warrior stood up to speak but was cut short. From the forest came a cry like a wolf's howl. A crowd of chiefs and warriors swarmed into the lodge, leading a prisoner. Uncas!

Someone grabbed the Mohican by the arm and shoved him forward. Heyward mingled with the others as they took their places. When all were seated, the gray-haired village chief spoke.

"Mohican," he said. "You have proved your courage. We do not ask your name. You may rest until dawn, then you will learn your fate."

The Indians bound their captive, then slowly left the lodge. Heyward found himself alone with Uncas, who whispered to him, "Gray Head and my father are safe, and Hawkeye's rifle does not sleep. Go now."

Heyward wandered about the village, searching for some trace of Alice. Finally, he went back to the council lodge. There, he found the warriors smoking peacefully.

THE FAKE MEDICINE MAN

No sooner had Heyward seated himself than a chief spoke to him in French. "I thank the Great White Father of Canada for sending you. An evil spirit lives in the wife of one of my warriors. Can you frighten it away?"

Heyward, who knew something of the tricks of medicine men, nodded.

Before anything more could be said, a warrior strode into the lodge and sat down beside Heyward.

Magua! Heyward felt his spine tingle with fear, but the Huron never even glanced at him. Instead, the Huron smoked in silence, staring at the prisoner whose back was toward him.

Uncas suddenly turned and met Magua's gaze. The Huron's eyes narrowed, then gleamed with ferocious joy. "It is Uncas, our great enemy!" he cried.

"Die, Mohican!" Magua lifted his tomahawk, then dropped it. "No – let us wait until morning. Let the squaws see him tremble!"

At this, the warriors bound Uncas more tightly and took him away. The chief who had asked for Heyward's help beckoned to the fake medicine man, and the two left the lodge. The sun was setting as they made their way through dense trees to a grassy clearing at the foot of a small cliff. Heyward sensed a presence behind them, and turned to see a shadowy figure. A bear!

"Fear nothing," said the Huron chief. "This is the costume of our village witchdoctor. The bear spirit is good medicine." He walked up to the cliff face and pushed aside a bark door covering an opening.

With the bear at their heels, they walked into a rock chamber lit by firelight and divided by stone partitions. The sick woman lay unconscious on a pile of Indian blankets, surrounded by squaws. To Heyward's amazement, there stood David Gamut, playing the flute!

The music master's eyes widened with terror when he saw the bear. Forgetting his disguise, he blurted out, "She's nearby!" and darted out of the cave.

A Friendly Bear

The chief ordered the women to leave. "Brother," he said to Heyward, "treat this squaw well. I will go now." A moment later, Heyward was alone with the sick woman and the bear.

"What shall I do now?" muttered the major worriedly. As he spoke, the bear raised its front paws and began tugging at its head. A smiling face appeared. It was Hawkeye!

"Uncas and I were on our way to the Delaware camp where Magua took Cora," explained the scout. "Some Hurons attacked us. Uncas was captured, but I escaped and followed the Hurons' trail here. By a stroke of luck, I met the village witchdoctor in his costume. A tap on the head fixed him, and here I am!"

"I've looked everywhere for Alice," explained Heyward. "but I haven't found her. Did you hear what the music teacher said?"

"If she's here," replied Hawkeye, "we'll soon find her." He climbed up a stone partition and looked over. Heyward could see him making a signal to keep quiet to someone on the other side.

"She's back there," whispered Hawkeye.

Heyward leaped to his feet. Wiping off his medicine-man paint as best he could, so as not to frighten Alice, he hurried to her side.

"I knew you wouldn't desert me," Alice said, tears in her eyes. The young officer had no time to reply, for at that moment he felt a light tap on his shoulder. He spun around. Magua again! The Indian grinned wickedly.

At that instant, the bear suddenly grabbed Magua from behind.

"Well done!" cried Heyward, taking a rawhide cord and tying up Magua.

"Wrap Alice in this Indian blanket and follow me," ordered Hawkeye. "You'll say you've trapped the evil spirit in the cave and that we're taking the sick squaw into the forest." He put the bear's head on again, and they walked out of the cave with Alice.

A little group of people waited outside expectantly.

"The evil spirit has left your daughter and is now trapped inside the cave," announced Heyward. "I'm taking her into the woods to strengthen her with roots and herbs."

Heyward, followed by Hawkeye, marched off with Alice safely in his arms. Soon they were following a narrow trail.

"This path leads to a river," said Hawkeye. "Follow its banks until you reach a waterfall. You'll see the campfires of the Delaware village where Cora was taken. You'll be safe there."

"What about you?" asked Heyward.

"Uncas is the Hurons' prisoner. He needs my help," said the scout, turning back toward the village. On the outskirts, he noticed a tumbledown hut where a light glimmered. Going down on all fours, Hawkeye crept inside, only to find himself face to face with David Gamut! The terrified music master fumbled for his flute, thinking that music might tame the terrible bear.

"Put that flute away," Hawkeye ordered, tugging off his bear's head. "Can you show me where Uncas is?"

"Yes indeed," said Gamut. "Follow me."

Four or five warriors guarded the entrance to the lodge where Uncas was being held. When they saw Gamut and what looked like the village witchdoctor, they stepped aside.

"Off with you!" cried Gamut. "The Great Bear's spirit will put fear in the prisoner's heart, but might rob you of your courage!"

The Hurons' eyes widened, and they scurried away.

"Cut the Mohican's bonds," said Hawkeye to Gamut.

Uncas leapt to his feet. "Quick! Let us go to my grandfather's people, the Tortoise tribe," he whispered.

"Wait!" said Hawkeye. He took off the bear costume and gave it to Uncas. "Now," Hawkeye told Gamut, "you must sit in the shadow and pretend to be Uncas." The music master bravely agreed. Hawkeye and the bear slipped out of the lodge.

The trick was soon discovered. The guards left the trembling Gamut and rushed to the council lodge. Ten of the wisest chiefs were then sent to the cave. There, to their amazement, they found the dying squaw and, after a short search, the bound and gagged form of Magua.

The Huron was furious at the loss of Alice and the escape of Uncas. He was sure his victim and her rescuers were heading for the village where the Delawares, people of the Tortoise, lived. Cora was being held there as his prisoner, for one thing; also, he knew the Mohicans shared the tortoise symbol with the Delawares. This meant they would receive hospitality and a safe haven there.

Before dawn the next morning, a group of Huron warriors set off for the Delaware village. As they came near, Magua went on ahead.

The sun had already risen when the Huron entered the village. He was greeted by the village chief.

"The wise Huron is welcome among his brothers of the lakes," said the chief.

"I bring gifts for my brothers," replied Magua. "Have my brothers seen traces of the white man?"

"The moccasins of strangers have been in our lodges," replied the chief.

"Has my brother beaten off these dogs?" Magua asked.

"That would not be good," said the chief. "A stranger is always welcome."

"But these strangers are Magua's prisoners, and among them is Long Rifle!" protested the Huron.

"If that is true, your prisoners will be returned to you," the chief calmly replied. "We will assemble the tribal council and call upon the great chief, Tamenund."

By noon, a great throng had gathered in the open space in the center of the village. A hush fell as an ancient chief appeared. His face was covered with the fine tattoo marks of an earlier day. Two slightly younger chiefs walked slowly beside him as he passed through the seated crowd.

The great Tamenund ordered the strangers to be brought to him.

"Stand forward, whoever among you is Long Rifle," said Tamenund.

There was a pause, then the scout stepped forward. "I am the man whom my friends the Delawares call Hawkeye. It is the traitor Magua and his Hurons who call me Long Rifle."

"Where is this Magua?" asked the great chief.

"Here I am, friend Tamenund," said Magua boldly, standing up and striding into the center of the gathering.

"Friend?" said Tamenund, frowning. He stared at the Huron. "Are the Hurons rulers of the earth? What brings you here?"

"I have come to take what belongs to me!" cried Magua.

"The law of the Great Manitou is just, Huron," Tamenund replied quietly. "Take what belongs to you and leave!"

Magua beckoned Hawkeye and his friends to follow him, but Cora threw herself at Tamenund's feet.

"Wise and just Delaware chief, have pity!" she cried. "Our Indian friend is one of your people. Please listen to him!"

"Let him come forward," ordered the chief.

Uncas, last of the Mohicans, slowly walked up to the chief.

"What language does this prisoner speak?" asked Tamenund.

"The language of the people of the Tortoise," replied Uncas.

"How could a Delaware come unrecognized into the camp of his own people? Your heart is hiding some lie!" said Tamenund severely.

Uncas bared his chest. There, plain for all to see, was the tattoo of a tortoise. It was blue – the symbol of the Mohicans, one of the greatest Delaware families.

"Who are you?" asked Tamenund in amazement.

"Uncas, son of Chingachgook," replied the prisoner.

"The hour of Tamenund is near!" exclaimed the old chief, tears of joy in his eyes. "The Great Manitou has sent a grandson to fill my place. Uncas, the last of the Mohicans, has been found!"

The young warrior bowed his head respectfully, then raised it.
"The Huron is a traitor," he said.

Magua walked up to the old Indian. "Tamenund the Just will not
keep what belongs to a Huron," he said.

Tamenund turned to Uncas. "Has this Huron any rights over you?
Has he won a battle?"

"He has no rights, wise Tamenund!" replied Uncas.

"What about the fair-haired woman?"

"She can go free," said Uncas.

"And the dark-haired woman that the Huron left with my warriors?" asked Tamenund.

"She is mine!" cried Magua. "Mohican, you know she is mine."

"My grandson is silent," remarked Tamenund.

"He is right," murmured Uncas.

Tamenund thought for a moment then asked one of his tribesmen, "Is this Huron a chief?"

"He is a leader of his tribe," was the answer.

"Woman," said Tamenund, turning toward Cora, "a great warrior wants you for his bride. You must follow him."

The gloating Magua strode up to Cora and grabbed her arm.

"Huron," said Uncas, "before the sun touches the trees, there will be men on your trail."

"Hah! Rabbits more likely. I spit on you!" retorted Magua, and he marched off into the forest, protected by the unbreakable laws of Delaware hospitality.

Uncas watched Cora leave with Magua, then silently made his way through the crowd and entered his lodge.

ON THE WARPATH

The Delawares didn't wait long to respond to Magua's insult. As the sun touched the tops of the trees, Uncas came out of his lodge and struck his tomahawk deep into the village war post. A great cry went up from all the warriors of the assembled tribe. They would punish the Huron and free the girl!

The Delaware warriors, with Hawkeye and Heyward among them, made their way swiftly and silently through the woods. Before long, they came upon the music teacher making his escape from the Huron village.

"Tell us what you know about the Hurons," whispered Hawkeye.

"Those heathens are hiding in the forest between here and the village, and you'd better go straight back where you came from!"

"What about Magua?" asked Uncas.

"He's with them. And so was Cora, but he left her in a cave and ran off, mad as a hornet, to lead the savages."

"Give me twenty warriors," said Hawkeye to Uncas. "You must go along the river and join Colonel Munro and Chingachgook."

THE AMBUSH

Hawkeye's party wound through the trees in single file. Before long, the sound of gunshot filled the air behind them, and a Delaware dropped to the ground.

"I feared as much," Hawkeye cried. "Take cover, men!"

The battle raged through the undergrowth. The more numerous Hurons were beginning to surround the Delawares, when suddenly the sound of a new rifle was heard.

"Chingachgook speaks!" shouted Hawkeye as loudly as he could. The effect on the Hurons was instantaneous, and they scattered like ants.

Uncas sped through the forest, leading nearly a hundred warriors, hot on the heels of Magua and his band. The Hurons reached the village and turned to fight with desperate fury.

Magua, realizing that all was lost, slipped away from the battle with two of his men.

Sharp-eyed Uncas raced after the fugitives with Hawkeye, Major Heyward, and Gamut close behind. Magua darted swiftly into the cave where Cora was held prisoner. Before the rescuers could do anything, he rushed out again, dragging the girl behind him. The Huron climbed onto a rocky ledge above a deep canyon, followed by his two companions.

"I'll go no further," screamed Cora, trying to pull free.

Magua pulled out a knife and turned to the prisoner. "Choose, woman," he said. "My wigwam or death!"

He raised the weapon, but in that moment a cry rang out, and Uncas jumped down from a rock high above them. At the same instant, one of Magua's warriors stabbed Cora in the heart.

With a blood-curdling scream, Magua plunged his dagger into the Mohican's back as he landed.

Uncas stumbled forward, arm raised, and drove his knife into the breast of Cora's killer before collapsing at Magua's feet. The enraged Huron stabbed Uncas savagely in the breast three times. The last of the Mohicans lay lifeless on the ledge, his heart pierced.

"Hah!" shouted the Huron, giving a cry of victory. But his triumph was shortlived, for Hawkeye suddenly appeared a few feet above him, rifle raised.

"Paleface dog!" screamed Magua scornfully, racing along a ledge and hurling himself desperately across a wide gap. Hawkeye's rifle thundered. Just as the Huron was about to grasp at the rocks on the far side, his body stiffened, and he fell headlong into the canyon.

A SAD ENDING

The following day the Delaware tribe was in mourning.

The brave and generous-hearted Cora, shrouded in sacred beaver and Indian robes, lay upon a bier.

At the foot of the bier sat Colonel Munro, his head in his hands. Gamut was standing to one side as Alice sobbed softly.

Beside Cora's funeral bier was the body of Uncas, prepared for burial in the Indian fashion and decorated with precious ornaments. The corpse was placed sitting up, as though alive. In front of Uncas' body stood Chingachgook, Hawkeye, and Tamenund.

The old chief prayed to the Great Manitou. Then one of the other chiefs gave a signal to six Indian maidens, who formed a ring around Cora's body. They lifted the bier onto their shoulders and walked away slowly, chanting mournfully in honor of the young white girl who had died so bravely and gone to the heaven of the palefaces.

Munro and the others followed the procession. The place chosen for Cora's burial was a small mound among a grove of young pine trees.

The Indian maidens placed Cora's body in a birch-bark coffin. As they lowered it into its final resting place, the music master sang a simple hymn.

The body of young Uncas was placed facing the rising sun. In his hands were weapons of war and of the hunt. Uncas was ready for the final voyage to the land of his fathers. The Delawares paid tribute to his bravery with sorrowful cries.

Chingachgook lifted his head and spoke for the first time during the long ceremony. "Why do my brothers mourn? Is it because a young warrior has gone to the happy hunting grounds, or that a brave and good chief has ended his days with honor? The Great Manitou needed a brave warrior, and has called him to his side. Now I am alone."

"No, Chingachgook," said Hawkeye, clasping his old friend's arms. "You are not alone. We may be of different races, but God has placed us so that we journey on the same path. Uncas was your son and my comrade. He has left us for a time, but you are not alone, my friend. Hawkeye, your brother, is here!"

THE END

© 1992 Dami Editore, Italy
Illustrated by Libico Maraja
Text by Jane Brierley and
Timothy Brierley, based on
an adaptation by Maria Danesi
and Anna Casalis

Published in 1994 by
Tormont Publications Inc.
338 Saint Antoine St. East
Montreal, Canada H2Y 1A3

ISBN 2-89429-589-8

Printed in EEC, Officine Grafiche De Agostini - Novara 1994
Bound by Legatoria del Verbano S.p.A.

Eugene Bondenko

valentyna Bondenko